T0062308

Gentlemen Callers

Corinne Hoex

GENTLEMEN CALLERS

Translated from the French by Caitlin O'Neil

DALKEY ARCHIVE PRESS

Dallas / Dublin

Library of Congress Cataloging-in-Publication Data available
upon request
ISBN: 978-1-628973-68-6

Support for the publication of this book has been provided by
the Fédération Wallonie Bruxelles.

FÉDÉRATION
WALLONIE-BRUXELLES

Dalkey Archive Press
Dallas/Dublin
www.dalkeyarchive.com

Table of Contents

Good Lord! What a large bed you have! Are you expecting company?

—Eugène Labiche

The Gas Station Attendant

He was simple in his dress, meticulously clean, and smelt of primrose soap.

—Anatole France, *Little Pierre*

Tonight, I dreamed of my gas station attendant. He'd fallen for me, and was lathering my car. I was sitting behind the steering wheel, and he, outside, was rubbing in wide arcs. His sponge foamed, foamed, and with this foam, he covered the roof, the doors, the windows.

I could no longer see anything. I was cut off from the world. All around me, I felt the hands of my attendant rubbing, circling that wet sponge over the body of the car.

Suddenly, my attendant was next to me in the seat. We were both hidden from sight, sheltered under the thick white foam.

The other vehicles were honking, honking, waiting behind us in line for the pump. But the attendant and I were invisible. And I liked the scent of the soap on his wet hands.

I dreamed of my attendant, and nothing will ever be the same. When I saw him this morning at the gas station and he asked me, "Want me to do your windshield?" I had such a brutal desire to be a sponge, a sponge in his hand, and I felt the shock of

3

the bucket's icy water when he plunged me in before
stroking me over the window.

The Swimming Instructor

The octopus has no mass of muscle, no threatening cry, no armor, no horn, no sting, no pincers, no tail with which to seize or batter its enemies, no sharp-edged fins, no clawed fins, no spines, no sword, no electric discharge, no virus, no poison, no claws, no beak, no teeth. And yet of all animals the octopus is the one that is most formidably armed.

What, then, is the octopus? It is a suction pad.

—Victor Hugo, *The Toilers of the Sea*

Since early fall, I've been regularly attending the pool on Perch Street where Max, the swimming instructor, in his vermilion Lycra bathing suit, cut very high up on his thighs, practices the backstroke.

I like the backstroke. I've likewise dedicated myself to it. One day, with practice, I'll become this sculpted swimmer with long, tapered legs, who swims with Max in my dreams.

However, tonight, as I head toward the large pool:

"Don't go in! Don't go in!" my swimming instructor panics, emerging abruptly from the pool, water streaming from his limbs, to run to me over the wet tiles. "Don't go in there! It's full of octopuses! And they're ferocious, especially with other women! No, don't get in! They're insanely jealous! They'll devour you!"

And, advancing toward me in his molded Speedo:

"With me, of course, it's different," Max confesses in my ear. "They know me. And also, I'm a man," he flatters himself, snapping the elastic waistband of his dripping suit. "I know how to handle them. Want to see?"

Then, standing against me, so close that his chest brushes mine, and his athletic hips, and his muscular thighs, and his appealing suit, my swimming instructor, with his large palms, very slowly, with delicious lightness, caresses my arms, softly caresses, from my wrists to my shoulders, from my shoulders to my wrists, softly caresses.

Under his light touch, my arms lengthen and stretch, divide, unfurl, sharpen dizzyingly, sense new audacities germinating inside them—unruly, brazen, they ripple and wave against Max's chest, wrap around his waist, clasp his hips, palpate his scarlet suit under their suckers, explore the delights of modern textiles, savor the incomparable qualities of elastane and Lycra.

Facing me, at the edge of the pool, their heads half out of the water, some twenty octopuses are watching me, glaring.

The Furrier

Fruits pure of outrage, by the blight unsmitten,
With firm, smooth flesh that cried out to be bitten.
> —Charles Baudelaire, *The Flowers of Evil*

Monsieur Kremer, the furrier, was asleep beside me last night. This was convenient because my feet were cold, and it was warm between his thighs.

In order not to wake Monsieur Kremer, I proceeded cautiously, first venturing the tip of my toe, then, taking great care, I slipped further in until my entire foot was deep within his warmth.

I was about to achieve my goal, both feet nestled in the tender heat of Monsieur Kremer's inner thighs, when:

"Did you think I wouldn't notice? You're completely frozen!" protested the sleepy voice of the furrier.

I immediately feared for my dream, the warmth of which was threatening to dissipate. So my frozen feet, not lacking in guile, very quickly became two charming fur animals, two river otters whose opulent pelts Monsieur Kremer, I knew, was familiar with. And the furrier, reassured, slept anew in a happy slumber, leaving his two visitors to hunt as they wished.

These two otters were, truth told, quite nibbling and biting creatures, ferocious little beasts with needle-sharp teeth and cool tongues, aggressive, carnivorous, and entirely determined, it seemed, to avenge their late sisters whose naphthalene-embalmed skins lay at rest as muffs, stoles, and fur-lined coats in the company of an opossum collar and a foxtail in the window of *Martin Kremer Furrier*.

These two Pasionarias, intractable, fanatical, escaped more and more wildly out of my control, refusing to release their prey.

Monsieur Kremer, however, didn't seem in a hurry to wake. I heard him emit several quiet drunken moans, small gasps—sensual, pleasurable—which only further excited the little creatures.

My frozen feet had come back to life, sated and satisfied.

The Baker 1

*At midnight, she was still working on the petits fours,
in silent despair at not being able to polish them all off.*

—Émile Zola, *The Earth*

I couldn't see the green eyes of Guillaume, my baker, because it was dark in my room, but I knew it was him because of the sweet, rich taste of pastry cream.

Guillaume held in his hand a very special cake that filled me with hunger, a cake swollen with a generous endowment of whipped filling that I had just stolen a lick of. I wanted to turn on the bedside lamp to see this cake better. But it was too late: I'd become a housefly. I buzzed around Guillaume, who chased after me, laughing.

"I told you, Madame! It's a new recipe! I don't know the side effects yet!"

Guillaume was fighting through the curtains to catch me. I playfully came and went, alighted on his temple, flitted over his nose, perched on his lip, stationed myself at the base of his neck, then took off again, flying above him, thrumming voluptuously. And my baker, jumping, leaping, was enjoying his pursuit.

"I warned you!" he protested with a crazed and impatient laugh, turning his head in every direction to follow my flight. "But you're so insatiable!"

Guillaume exploded with laughter, mocking me.

But I held out. I came to rest high up on the wall, I kept quiet, I feigned sleep. I could feel my pursuer, his senses heightened, approaching on tiptoe, reaching out his hand, ready to seize me. Then I sped to the opposite side of the room where I improvised an alluring and provocative buzz purely for his benefit.

He was searching for me. I kept quiet. I flew back, on a whim, to hum in his ear. All of a sudden, I dove on him, crawling under his shirt, tasting him, my wings quivering gently; titillating his nipples with the tips of my slender little feet, I teased him, tickled him. Guillaume, exasperated, laughed more than ever.

"Madame! Stop this foolishness!"

Every so often, I surreptitiously returned for yet another taste of his cake. I continued to suck at that frothy, whipped filling whose side effects I didn't want to wear off.

Then Guillaume crept up on me from behind.

"Just wait until I catch you, Madame! If it's cream you want, then cream you shall have!"

The Baker 2

She [. . .] came again, ten times, to pass by the almond cakes, St. Honoré cakes, savarins, flans, fruit tarts, platters of babas, eclairs, and cream puffs.

—Émile Zola, *The Belly of Paris*

Guillaume, the baker, paid me another visit. I was no longer a housefly, and he was happy. However, he admitted, he missed the tickle of my feet, the light touch of my wings, my intoxicating humming. He especially missed my proboscis, that thrilling proboscis that sucked his cream so expertly, so greedily.

And Guillaume's eyes, full of wistful reverie, smiled at that memory.

"For that," I told him, "you should have brought that cake again, you know, the one from last time, that serendipitous delight, filled with that delectably rich whipped cream. You should have brought that cake, that creative success, that culinary innovation, that rich rarity, instead of this stupid baba, this huge baba that's so copiously, so heavily soaked with rum, it's hit me under the wing."

"All the better, Madame!" concludes Guillaume with a triumphant laugh, malicious, sardonic. "It's hit you under the wing? Excellent! Perfect! Finally I've caught you!"

The Tailor

Let us rend, shred all these vain ornaments [. . .]

—Jean Racine, *Esther*

Tonight, I find myself in a tailor's fitting room, facing the triptych mirror whose self-reflections multiply my image and send it infinitely back to me.

I'm clothed in a full-skirted gown of amaranth taffeta with a sumptuous décolletage, a nervous taffeta, whispering, that shivers excitedly against my throat with each palpitation of my breath. My hands are gloved in black leather, a buttery leather, soft, that intimately hugs my slender fingers. My levantine silk heels sink into the thick fur of the rug.

I stand tall, immobile, my head held high. I'm waiting for the tailor. My heart pounds.

Then he's there. Out of nowhere, he appears. Around his neck, his measuring tape. On his arm, his pincushion. In his hand, his steel shears.

"You'll see, Madame," he announces to me, impatient, impassioned—his scissors sparkle under the chandelier—"You'll see, my dear Madame, you'll be amazed. The ensemble is a marvel."

I contemplate myself, perplexed. Am I not already dressed, luxuriously so? Could anything in the world exist as becoming, as desirable as the gown I'm already wearing? What could the most adept tailor do for me when I'm enrobed in this red taffeta?

Then the tailor unravels.

"Let's begin!" he decides, launching himself at me. And, with a decisive slice of his icy shears, with a voracious rasp, he violently rips my bodice, slits the taffeta of my dress from top to bottom, lacerates the scarlet silk like a bloodied pelt.

My reflections in the mirrors brace themselves against this rapacious onslaught. But the tailor is already attacking my slip, ripping off my undergarments, slicing my corset, peeling, stripping away my lingerie to the very last ribbon.

I'm naked in the glass. Dressed only in my black gloves. The tailor smiles over my shoulder.

"There we are, Madame. Your new finery. I daresay I've created a masterpiece."

I'm speechless, my feet lost among the shreds of my gown.

"Don't move!" the tailor orders. "I still have to ensure everything's perfect."

Pressing close to me, armed with his pins, diligent, meticulous, the tailor pricks here, pricks there, my hip, my neck, the tip of my breast. Blood beads. My skin crackles. I jump.

"Don't move, Madame! Don't interrupt me!" the tailor barks.

Continuing his work, absorbed in his creation, the tailor, with studied concentration, reviews his measurements, verifies the alignment of my throat, the soft curve of my thighs. With the tip of his chalk pencil, he marks the base of my neck and my collar bones, accentuates my bust, traces the slope of my lower back. With each stroke, I feel the cold, slippery pressure of the chalk. My stomach flutters. My skin trembles. I stave off even the smallest shiver.

Finally the tailor steps away, considers my reflection.

"It's perfect, don't you think, my dear Madame? The cut is remarkable. There's nothing to take in. Maybe a final touch if you'll allow me . . ."

And, with a nimble, searching hand, the tailor quickly tousles my pubic hair.

"How do you feel about this little dishevelment, Madame? I suggest just a light touch, very gamine. Would you prefer it thicker? Teased, perhaps? More exuberant? Just say the word, Madame. It's my job."

While the tailor musses and smooths, snarls and unsnarls, tangles and untangles, pushing his enviable skill to achieve the carefully slapdash look so admired in today's fashion, the mirrors, a hundred times, a thousand times, the mirrors caress me.

The Aviator

[. . .] a foretaste of the heavens' beatitude.

— Louis Bourdaloue, *Pensées*

Tonight, I'm christening my new duvet of swans' down, as welcoming as a soft cloud. It transports me to the open sky.

Here I am, bare, my rosy body a cloud among the clouds, drifting, vaporous, abundant. A charming female cumulus floating aimlessly in the azure air.

Then I hear the far-off sound of an engine, a faint roar that grows louder as it approaches.

Suddenly, there he is, beside me. An aviator in his scarlet single-seater, dazzling under the sun. A handsome aviator, bronzed and smiling, leather goggles, chinstrap helmet, red scarf blowing in the wind. He's a bit of a show-off, actually, quite the poseur, but insanely seductive and so brazen, so daring, so bold!

Behind the controls of his machine, followed by a cool, white plume, he circles me, brushing through my curves as he passes. Already, I feel myself beginning to yield.

He circles back, the red scarf flapping like a banner in the wind. He flies overhead, dives, rises again, falls in a tailspin, then regains altitude. His cockpit convulses. His fuselage rattles. My aerial mounds roll and shift in the blue sky, on lusty offer.

He circles back again, with audible joy. He banks steeply, scales me, takes me front and back. His propeller spins in a frenzy, the blades relentlessly whipping. My diaphanous thighs wrap around him. My bosom enfolds him. I'm a churning mist courted so gallantly, with such ardor, a distinctive exuberance. A mist, replete, pink with pleasure, penetrated with acrobatic artistry.

And again he circles back, like a drunken hornet, looping, climbing, spiraling, each time returning to me, each time passing through me. His entire hull trembles. His ailerons shudder, his levers shake.

I gather myself, soft, pillowy, I curl my loving tendrils around him. I expand, thicken, condense. A cloud cover heavy with a sweet, damp scent. A writhing mist, vapor suspended, whose raindrops—oh God!—are ready to fall!

The Mailman

As Boniface the postman left the post office he discovered that his round that day would not take as long as usual, and felt a sharp pleasure in the knowledge.

—Guy de Maupassant, "Old Boniface's Crime"

I dreamed of my mailman. He delivered his holiday greetings and offered me the traditional postal calendar. He had several of them in his bag, and they were stuck to each other. So he licked a finger and separated them. And I sensed that this was a man practiced in peeling back layers, a man well-versed in envelopes.

Since then, I've been a love letter. I've thrown myself into his bag. I feel the swing of his steps, and I hear his hobnail boots on the cobblestone streets.

Tonight, when he finishes his route, he'll find me at the bottom of his bag, quivering.

His fingers will at last be on me before they slide inside and open me.

The Museum Guard

Never let yourself be kissed by a man without a moustache; his kisses have no flavour, none whatever! They no longer have the charm, the mellowness and the snap—yes, the snap—of a true kiss. The moustache is the spice.

—Guy de Maupassant, "The Moustache"

I adore the arts. I visit the museum every week. My guard awaits me there. The guard of my dreams.

Unlike his colleagues, who were glued to their seats, stupefied with boredom, following my movements with a listless eye, he, upon seeing me, runs to me, smiling, smoothing his thumb over his trim, ginger moustache, and bows to kiss my hand.

This man, in my eyes, is a prince, gallant, irresistible, a prince enamored with the arts who welcomes me into his extensive gallery. Regardless of the unflattering cut of his uniform, my guard—my prince—is the most attractive of men.

The moustache figures significantly in the affair. A short, dense, deliciously tickly moustache that very precisely festoons his upper lip and whose prickliness enhances the smooth softness of his mouth. *This* is the pleasurable spice of the kiss. *This* is the genius of it. *This* is what electrifies me. *This*, so spry and seductive, that arouses a shiver as it brushes my skin.

Each week, as I mount the museum's imposing steps, I don't yet know which room I'll find my guard in. As soon as I see him, my heart jumps.

Already his lips draw near, eager, attentive. His breath caresses me. But the moustache first, the moustache excites me, arousing that divine simmer on the back of my hand.

Despite the deserted rooms and their promise of discretion, my guard, strangely, limits himself to that single kiss on the hand. One single kiss, but one kiss absolute. A virtuosic kiss. A kiss inspired. Because—depending on the room, the century, the painter—my guard confers upon each kiss a specific flavor, a delectable freshness whose sophistication and novelty are inspired by those of the artist.

Before a Hieronymus Bosch, the moustache will bristle, sharp and glinting. The teeth beneath the bristle will venture quick nips. The eyes will project flashes of light. And in his eyes, my own will tremble terribly.

Near a Botticelli, the lips will surrender themselves to my hand, full of reverie. The moustache grows tender, silky, melancholic, delivering a languorous ecstasy.

In the Rubens hall, in front of the overflowing flesh, the bared throats, the kiss will be enthusiastic, the moustache impassioned, and it will express all of the painter's vigor.

Alas, for a while now, my guard has been stationed in the abstracts hall. His kiss is suffering the effects: distant and cerebral. His expression is withdrawn, smile extinguished, lips sullen. The moustache is anxious, off-kilter. One day soon it will surely disappear altogether, shaved off.

For several weeks, I'll no longer dream of my guard. My nights will abandon the museum. I'll wait, dreaming of our former pleasures, our exquisite indiscretions, our exhilarating rendezvous under Bosch, under Rubens. I'll wait for the moustache to grow back.

The Butcher

It's the tango of the butchers of la Villette
It's the tango of the slaughterhouse killers
Come don the ruffles and cauls of their set
And sip on blood in the setting sun.

May blood run.

—Boris Vian, "The Joyous Butchers"

A butcher. He has a knife that cuts well, parting flesh as raw and as bloody as the women of his dreams.

Behind the storefront shutter, within the white-tiled walls, alone with me in his shop, he prepares my beef tenderloin.

He's standing at his butcher's block. His apron bloodies his thighs. In the shop window, on the chilled marble, next to the pallid tongues and glandulous livers, dream the deep rosy brains of two adjacent calves' heads.

The butcher is immersed in his work. I watch his firm fingers, his short-clipped nails, his thick wrists. I appreciate his precision, his confident movements, the attentive, almost tender way he thrusts his blade, stripping the meat from the bone, pulling away the tendons. His sharp knife incises and slices cleanly. The flesh bares itself before him and allows itself to be penetrated. A bright shiver runs through me, a sharp pleasure, impeccably honed, that flirts with the threshold of pain.

The butcher continues his work, trims his cuts, covers his scale with a sheet of waxed paper, smooth like percale, and into its center he tosses the cut of beef, which surrenders limply.

He finally raises his head, his dark eyes on me.

And when he asks, "Anything else I can do for you today?" I feel as though there is.

The Groomer

From its fair and dark fur
Comes a scent so gentle, that one night
I was caught in its balm, by having
Caressed it once, only once.

—Charles Baudelaire, *The Flowers of Evil*

A groomer sets me in the center of a silk cushion facing him on an intricately inlaid dresser. No, what am I saying? Not a dresser, more like an altar where rare incense burns before me, wrapping me in its scent. Upturned nose, haughty whiskers, I consent to breathe the soporific vapors.

He carefully works his brush through my tangles. His movements are filled with reverence for my fur, my thick mysterious fur, my smoke-blue fur flecked sumptuously with silver. Thus, attentive, considerate, he brushes me. Humbly, he brushes me. Gradually, though, his movements grow bolder. He plunges his exultant face into my coat, intoxicated with my warm scent.

I allow myself to be stroked. After all, isn't that why I've turned into a cat tonight, a Persian pussy? I let myself be pet, I let myself be kissed, and, my eyes drowsy and slitted, I turn an indulgent turquoise look on my groomer.

There's no danger that I'll unsheathe my claws. My paws are pure velvet, and my sharp teeth hide harmlessly behind my innocently curved mouth. From time to time, a muffled purr slips out, difficult to hold in—I admit—with the shivers of pleasure that are running down my spine. I let out discreet trills as well, delicate, restrained, as befits a feline of my pedigree. I arch my back in one long motion, graceful and lithe, to meet each of the strokes that my groomer bestows upon me. Under his seeking lips, I stretch, elongate my body, I offer him my belly and its thick, enticing fluff. His long fingers knead me, tenderly tease my fur; his excitement grows, my shivers intensify.

Later, I know—because I know what he likes—my groomer will fetch his perfumes with great ceremony, will deliberate between amber, musk, benzoin, sandalwood, and, with the tip of his little finger, will carefully dab a trace of tuberose between my bewitching eyes.

He'll continue his ritual, opening his chest of jewels at my feet. His rubies, his pearls, his sapphires will shine, and he'll drape them over me as if adorning a goddess.

He'll sing my praises with loving endearments, will call me his "panther," his "tigress," and my fur will gleam with the sparkling gems.

But we're not there yet. For now, he's brushing me, smoothly, with devotion. In this moment still, luxuriously, my groomer is brushing me.

And while he brushes me, while I'm half-asleep, purring, my eyes closed, I dream blissfully, rapturously, I dream . . . that I am a woman.

The Young Priest 1

Each of us had a small armoire with a full ecclesiastical wardrobe: a black cassock with a long train, an alb, a surplice, black silk stockings, two zucchetti [. . .] rabats trimmed with small white pearls, all that was necessary.

— Alphonse Daudet, *Little Good-for-Nothing*

Several days ago, a church camp started up in the space below my apartment, overseen by a priest, young and spritely, who manifests in my dreams by night.

He arrives with a vigorous stride, cassock flapping behind him, his entourage following on his heels, greets me with his hungry smile, transfixed with shy desire, sliding his shining eyes briefly to my thighs, then sends his unruly escort to wait on the other side of the door and moves closer to me, bashful yet brash.

But I'm asleep. I'm fast asleep. If I weren't, the young priest would flee, taking with him the gleeful little troop stamping and snorting on my landing.

"You're Saint Theresa," he murmurs, his catechistic voice above me, "Bernini's Saint Theresa, and no matter what I do, you remain solid marble. All saints are tried and tested in that. That's the reason they're canonized."

The young priest then frees himself from his cassock, which he leaves in a black pile at the foot of the bed, and I kneel on my white cloud, back arched, face upturned, lips parted, surrendering my flesh to the Redeemer. I do my best to remain insensate.

Thus, thanks to the young priest's intercession, the Holy Spirit enters me. God clasps me in His arms, possesses me with His mouth, radiates His light by waking the wild urges of his servant's potent sap.

Panting, feverish, lashed with desire, I obediently receive the visit from On High.

Behind the door I hear the agitated crowd, waiting and scuffling.

The Young Priest 2

How pleasant and sweet to behold brethren fervent and devout, well-mannered and disciplined!

—Thomas à Kempis, *The Imitation of Christ*

Tonight, the young priest approaches me once again. Still full of spirit. Still full of play.

"Saint Theresa was very good," he says to me with a calibrated pout. "But she's not the only one. There's also Saint Catherine. We haven't done Saint Catherine. And there's Saint Ursula. And Saint Barbara. We have to try Saint Barbe. Saint Barbe's very, very good. The kids in the camp love that one. And Saint Agnes. Saint Agnes is also very good. Very popular with the ladies. Or Saint Amata of Assisi. Or Saint Margaret of Antioch. We absolutely, absolutely *must* try Saint Margaret of Antioch one of these nights. But you need to be in shape for that one! And there's Saint Zita too, not bad, but a little uncomfortable, especially for the woman. And Saint Euphemia of course, Saint Euphemia of Chalcedon. I haven't tried that one in a while, but I should mention that the last time . . ."

What stamina the Church has! Such admirable convictions! And to think that there are those who claim its strength is waning.

The Circus Trainer

. . . to drown in the abyss—heaven or hell,
Who cares? Through the unknown, we'll find the new.
—Charles Baudelaire, *The Flowers of Evil*

"Why do you never dream about me?" asked Herbert, the circus trainer. "I'm a handsome man, after all. Look at my red jacket. My fringed epaulettes. My gold brandenburgs. And my boots? My tall, scarlet boots? Go on, make an effort! Dream of me!"

Herbert certainly makes big claims! There he is, parading himself in the middle of the ring under the trusting watch of his ten lovable sea lions, his ten docile pinnipeds with handsome smiling faces that, vibrissae trembling, follow him seriously with their large, damp eyes. He doesn't doubt himself for a minute! The world is his oyster! What he wants, he demands!

"Make an effort! Dream of me!"

Of course, Herbert! You only had to ask! I dream on command. Soon, with some practice, I'll be spinning a ball on my nose, I'll waddle from one side of the ring to the other, I'll haul myself, fat and slick, onto one of your red and yellow stands, and I'll applaud Herbert wildly, clapping my flippers at his entry into the ring.

Since, in spite of a persistent odor of herring,

dear Herbert—I'm forced to admit—does boast several physical advantages, I did what I could last night, after all was said and done. Honestly, I tried. I thought very hard of the gold brandenburgs and the red boots. And I was almost there. I brushed against Herbert in my dream. Then it veered off course. Only slightly, but all the same . . . It wasn't Herbert.

Instead, I swam alongside an elephant seal. I was under it. Against it. Stomach to stomach. My bare skin flush against its thick pelt. I had taken the precaution of tucking my hair into my shower cap because the huge, wild animal liked to dive deep.

The animal seemed to welcome my presence graciously with supple twirls and, very considerately, resurfaced from time to time so that I could take a breath. I did my part by holding on with all my strength and keeping my chest glued to the animal's belly.

An elephant seal is remarkably refreshing. You leave feeling completely revitalized. Much more so than with a circus trainer in a tailcoat with brandenburgs, even if he is shod in scarlet boots.

The Schoolteacher

That afternoon, during the four o'clock recess, he approached me and handed me, still smiling, still silent, the handbook opened to page 12: The Teacher's Responsibilities to the Students.

—Alphonse Daudet, *Little Good-for-Nothing*

A stare, blue, piercing, penetrated me that night, and it was at the same time exquisite and excruciating, as if a wooden ruler were pressing down the length of my spine.

I recognized Monsieur Pirodin, my schoolteacher, standing at the foot of the bed, smiling at me mischievously as he stroked his goatee, his eyes glinting behind his round wire-framed glasses.

I suddenly felt the apprehension, the anxiety that had seized me as a child, as under this same sharp look, bent over my notebook, I'd labored to form perfect letters. With the tip of his metal ruler, Monsieur Pirodin would raise my chin: "Sit up straight!" With that forced movement, my hand shook, my pencil slipped. I'd have to redo the whole page. Monsieur Pirodin didn't accept any mistakes.

But that night, in my bedroom, Monsieur Pirodin fixed me with a sly, knowing look, delectably presenting to me a piece of white chalk, a beautiful gleaming stick.

Monsieur Pirodin and his chalk seemed to be connected by a joyful complicity. Holding me in thrall, he twirled it around and around in his fingers, fondling it lovingly, caressing it with desire, and above it he was peering at me, his eyes shimmering with malicious anticipation.

Suddenly, he took a decisive step toward the blackboard.

"Let's begin!" he snapped with a fierce look.

His pupils shone with diabolic light.

And so, Monsieur Pirodin pressed his chalk to the blackboard and, his fingers tensed as his nails bit into the brittle mineral, his demonic blue eyes still dominating mine, he ground the chalk against the smooth surface very slowly, millimeter after torturous millimeter, in an intolerable and delicious screech, crossing the blackboard with one magnificent white line.

I cried out in my sleep, one long, hoarse shriek. A breathless fever pitch.

The Tradesman

This cool spring, and its waters silver-clean,
In gentle murmurs seem to tell of love,
And all about the grass is soft and green;
And the close alders weave their shade above;

The sidelong branches to each other lean,
And as the west-wind fans them, scarcely move;
The sun is high in mid-day splendour sheen,
And heat has parched the earth, and soiled the grove.

Stay, traveller, and rest thy limbs awhile,
Faint with the thirst, and worn with heat and toil;
Where thy good fortune brings thee, traveller, stay.

Rest to thy wearied limbs will here be sweet,
The wind and shade refresh thee from the heat,
And the cool fountain chase thy thirst away.

—Philippe Desportes, "An Invitation"

It happened to me when I saw him, with his sturdy shoulders.

He was a tradesman. He was on a nearby jobsite, working on the foundation of a house. I'd heard the pinging of the pickaxe, the scrapes of the shovel.

The midday sun was voracious. I was sitting in the shade of the sycamores. He approached me.

"Mother of God, what a scorcher!"

He had the lilting accent of the South. His chest muscles rippled under his shirt.

"Good Lord, it's hot!"

I felt how warm he was, how thirsty he was. In the leafy canopy above us rasped the obsessive call of the cicadas.

He set down his pickaxe. His biceps were hypnotizing. I heard running water. It was me. I had become a fountain. A pleasant village fountain, surrounded by watercress and horsetails, and where sparrows sometimes stopped to quench their thirst. A modest fountain with neither marble basin nor sculpted Triton. A simple, babbling spray.

"Sweet Jesus, this water is cool."

He bent over me. He smiled at me, with his

velvety golden eyes, as he gazed at himself reflected in me. He took me in his large hands, lifted me to his mouth, and I felt his lips, and I felt his tongue. He seized me again, splashed me against his chest. I slid down the length of his neck, I soaked through his shirt, feeling my way over each muscle, winding toward his navel, trickling further and further.

I spent a long moment there, lost in my thoughts, fulfilled, evaporating leisurely. The cicadas in the branches were calling still more loudly.

Then he was gone. He grabbed his pickaxe and left.

From afar, I heard the stubborn blows begin again in the burning air. How hard my tradesman works! So vigorous! So strong! May he overheat again soon.

The Chiropractor

Here were exchanged a thousand burning kisses [. . .]
—Jean de la Fontaine, *Complete Tales in Verse*

"Are you asleep?"

Of course I'm asleep. Otherwise he wouldn't be in my dream with his mango-scented breath tickling my ear.

It's my chiropractor, Monsieur Herstel, in his white work shirt, tightly buttoned. He bends over me again.

"Hey, are you asleep?"

Obviously I'm asleep. Would he be addressing me so casually if I weren't?

"Are you asleep?"

Yes, it's alright. He shouldn't worry. I'm fast asleep. He can touch his feverish mouth and affectionate lips to the back of my neck. It's not a problem: I'm asleep. I won't remember.

"C5," Monsieur Herstel whispers shyly, placing a first kiss on my fifth cervical vertebra. "C6, C7," he continues as he descends.

From vertebra to vertebra, his lips creep further down. I feel him each time blow softly, with the sound of a kiss, then move down one and kiss again. Occasionally, I hear the faint sound of suction, precise, targeted, clinical.

"T1, T2, T3 . . . the charming thoracics," Monsieur Herstel continues with professionalism. "L3, L4, L5 . . . the lovable lumbars," he murmurs, muffled under the bedsheet. "You have a small blockage, a very small blockage," Monsieur Herstel observes, as he obligingly licks my transverse process. "A very small blockage," his voice slightly tipsy, distorted by the blankets confining it. "Don't move. I've reached your sacrum. I adore your coccyx. Ah, the tender coccyx! No, no, don't move! Go back to sleep, Madame."

The Cook

This girl could decorate a bed all right,
And, succulent, excite the appetite.

       —Jean de la Fontaine, *Complete Tales in Verse*

A betoqued cook is leaning over me.

"Mmmmm . . ."

I see him, joyful face, nostrils flared, the shining lips of a man with a healthy appetite, who knows the exquisite torment of whetting it.

"Mmmmm . . ."

He observes me simmering at the bottom of a large pot, submerged in a marinade of Côtes du Rhone, embellished with thyme, bay leaves, cloves, and carrots, cut in coins.

"Mmmm . . ."

Above me, I see him salivating and inhaling small wafts of steam. It pleases him. It lasts for hours. He never grows weary, never takes his eyes off me, and watches with fervent delight as this flesh melts into juicy tenderness.

My juices are frothing, bubbling, syrupy, thick.

"Let's see how it's going down there!" he finally decides.

And he lets the chilled tip of his knife sink in.

The Hunter

The trees in the forests are beautiful women
Whose unseen bodies live beneath the bark.
Their tresses are showered with purest waters and
Dried by wind that restores their shaded crowns.

—Pierre Louÿs, "The Trees of the Forests"

I'm a shaded forest. I have tall trees with dark roots, dense copses and murky old growth, ravines, undergrowth, nettles, and brambles. I have immense beech trees and proud oaks. I have clearings, too, gaps in the brush where the moon penetrates and caresses my moss. I have fairies, witches, ogresses, elves. I have divinities, nymphs, undines, and charming dryads lounging placidly within my canopy. And I have does, of course, and vixens, and ladybugs, damselflies, every sort of insect that crawls and that flies and that you can't even see. I am a forest inhabited by mystery, filled with the fluttering of wings, with silent flight, with whispered movements, with quivering, with animal cries. A forest alive with its humming, its uneasy hooting, its crazed calls.

Tonight, however, I'm a forest that stifles its murmurs, I restrain my birdsong, I repress my rustlings. Because tonight, I am an amorous forest, watching and waiting.

He's there. At my edge. He's not a botanist. He walks too quickly. He doesn't have that delicate way of using two fingers to pluck one of my Endymions, nor that delicious habit of brushing the fronds of my ferns as he passes. No, he's not a botanist. And in any case, he's not carrying a collecting box.

He's not a woodcutter either. He walks like a warrior, and he's not carrying an axe. What's that he's carrying over his shoulder, not a tool and vaguely threatening? A weapon? A gun! Our man is a hunter! He's in a hurry and presses forward, neck tensed—Onward!—straight ahead. He enters my dream without even a glance in my direction, with the insolence of a true hunter, crushes my hyacinths, tramples my primroses. He enters my dream without even seeing that it's a dream.

I block his progress with one of my low-hanging branches. He hits his forehead on it. Will he finally see me? My brambles thicken and cut him off. Now will he see me? I feel him as he roughly treads my paths—Onward! Onward! He inspects me and searches deep within me, excavates, furrows. I make myself dense, thick, full, impenetrable. I make myself luxurious, shadowy, tangled. My hunter grows fearful. My hunter tries to turn back. But my brush, my bushes, my thickets, my thorny shrubs bring him to a halt.

My hunter is lost. He knows he's my prisoner. Finally he slows his pace. Finally he surrenders. Finally his dragging footsteps softly stroke me.

He sets down his gun, removes his cartridge belt, pulls off his tall boots, stretches out in my undergrowth, rolls over my moss. He tastes its delight, its silk, its velvet, and the exquisitely damp warmth secreted within my wet earth. He stretches, groans, yawns, contemplates my foliage draping over him like glossy tresses, breathes its perfume and its dewy scent of life pervaded by the night. My dryads sigh from the treetops.

In the mute gleam of a white moonbeam, my indiscreet ferns unfurl to peer at him, my damselflies flit over him in their probing flight, and I feel his heart beating against me. From within my humus, from the depths of my peat, from below my roots, I feel the rumble of his life.

The Geographer 1

The King has given the Dauphin his directions [for his wedding night] in a very circumstantial manner, and devised a sort of geography, with which he has extremely amused the Court.

—Madame de Sévigné, *Letters*

"So, my darling, where are we tonight?'

He's a geographer. He's a bit batty. Sometimes he comes to visit me, spreads his large map across my bed, and scrutinizes it in an aroused state. In my sleep, I hear the impatient rustle of the paper as he smooths it.

"So, where are we?"

With him I travel all night along the meridians and the parallels, offering my bare body to oceans, deserts, glaciers, mountain ranges.

"For me, my dear, there's no question," he decides as he gestures to the map. "I'm this island."

He points his index finger to the middle of the Pacific, to a form with a jagged shoreline, deeply scalloped and surrounded by blue.

"I'm this island, this open hand," he continues with encouragement, "this hand with the soothing palm. Feel my fingers, my darling. Feel how they love you."

Dreamily, my geographer draws his nails down my back with delicious lightness, the infinite languor of the waves that lap his island.

"But my darling," he asks me while courteously nibbling my nipples, "with this body of yours, this body that's so vast, so generous, this prodigious, inexhaustible body, where shall we put you?"

And rolling with me over the enormous map, embracing me on Africa, on Asia, on Europe, experimenting on Madagascar, testing the Azores, tasting Spain and Italy, here and there, my geographer suddenly exclaims, as he reaches for my lower back:

"You're the Americas, of course! Yes, from Alaska to Cape Horn! Let's not be stingy! The Americas, that's you! You're the Americas! These strong Canadian shoulders! This Californian bosom! Your tapered Central America! The soft fullness of your Peru! Darling, it's obvious: you're the Americas!"

And my geographer, reveling in his profession, as he names each region he gallantly assigns me, greets with a tender titillation their ridges, their valleys, and their bodies of water. His digits dance along my small Uruguay, tease my Florida, fondle my Yucatan, savor the softness of my gentle Colombia, plunge into my Potomac and my Saint Lawrence. His sensuous fingertips follow my Mississippi, trail down my thigh, caress my Chile, reach my Tierra del Fuego, skim my Patagonia. His hand finally clambers back up to my Pennsylvania, winds its way gallantly through my Hudson Strait, strokes my Manitoba, tempts my Ontario, stalks my Nebraska, finds my Idaho.

"My darling! My darling! I've seen you in all your states. I love the Americas!"

The Geographer 2

The poor beautiful Madelonne is so penetrated by this biting cold that she begged me to make her excuses [. . .] Her chest, her ink, her quill, her thoughts, all are quite frozen; she assures you, however, that her heart is not [. . .]

—Madame de Sévigné, *Letters*

My geographer is back. He immediately unfolds his map, which I notice—my goodness—is rather crumpled. He must have intensified his studies since our last session.

I watch him for a moment as he looks for me, irritated not to find me among the Americas.

Finally, he sees me, half-naked in the snow, skin flushed with the cold, shivering and happy, surrounded by large reindeer with velvety noses.

His whole body shivers icily.

"Really, darling! Poor darling! The North Pole! That's completely arctic! Polar! Hyperborean! Plus, all of that's going to melt. You're halfway to floating between icebergs up there. My poor darling, be reasonable. This sea ice isn't for you. Come down. Come join me. The weather's divine down here. Come, now, leave the North!"

And to further persuade me, my geographer, with his numbed, pursed lips, meticulously, like a perfect cartographer, checking his coordinates, places several frosty kisses on my shoulders, on my stomach, on my breasts.

This geographic survey is boring me to exhaustion.

I let out a yawn. My geographer is offended, promptly abandons his business, and rolls up his useless map, mood fouled.

"Well then, my complete and utter darling, since my company seems to be a burden to you, enjoy yourself all alone on your ice floe!"

He leaves my bedroom, slamming the door. Good riddance! I hope he stays gone. But "alone"? Why "alone"? Did he not see the beautiful polar bear with its luminous coat waiting for me among the icebergs?

The Pirate

Night comes, a black pirate disembarking on the golden skies.

—Arthur Rimbaud, "First Communion"

A brig packed with arms and munitions drifts indolently under a leaden sun, an inert black pavilion.

It's the midday rest. The ship is filled with pirates, defeated by the heat and the rum, snoring, mouths open, swinging in their hammocks above their treasure chests overflowing with gold.

They're not particularly attractive boys, not exceptionally squeaky-clean. Even the quartermaster. Even the captain. Old. Dirty. Hideous. Vermin-ravaged. A collection of wooden legs and eye-patches. An array of horrible mugs.

Except for him. Him alone. A young privateer stretched out insolently at the prow of the ship, hands behind his head, reclining on the bowsprit six meters above the water, relaxing in not a shred of clothing, his charms on offer for all to see.

Unlike the others, he is ravishing, endowed with a superb body, luscious skin, and adorable stubble, newly sprouted.

I'm already imagining my nipples being gently abraded under his incipient beard, my lips navigating that divine chest so tenderly dusted with hair. I feel a small laugh tingle and flare inside my belly.

Alas, the handsome privateer is unaware of me. He remains stretched out, idle, imperturbable, the ring in his earlobe flashing in the sun. His powerful young arms know nothing of me.

I can't stand it. I have to be near him. I plunge into the sea, and I become a wave, a deep wave that sinks down, that sucks in, a muscular wave that gathers its strength, a lustful wave that grows and swells.

My pretty pirate suspects nothing, trusting this calm water unrippled by wind. But the wave climbs. The wave rises. I leap up, unfurling. I launch myself, escorted by thousands of small silver fish swimming at my crest. I throw myself onto him. I break, crash over him, spread over his body with a quiet, gentle hiss, a frothy whisper. I seep into every crevice, I lick him, lap him, in a salty passion.

Then, slowly, leaving him several ribbons of seafoam to remember me by, very slowly, with regret, I recede.

The Night Watchman

Soldiers and black eunuchs guarded those defended gates.

—Pierre Loti, *Aziyadé*

Squeezed into his black suit, chest straining, shoulders restricted, with his polished, pointed shoes and a thick silver chain on his wrist, it's the night watchman.

Thick neck, military haircut, he's there, stationed in front of my bedroom door, keeping watch, muscles tensed.

"At your service, Madame. Sleep well. You won't be disturbed."

Alas, the watchman did his job. In the morning, I congratulate him.

"I slept marvelously, thank you. But unfortunately, I didn't dream."

"As expected, Madame. When I'm here, no one enters, not even into your dreams."

The Explorer

She drags in her wake the mangled remains
Of the set-upon stag she'd devoured that night;
And over the moss flowers frightful stains,
Red and steaming still, shine in moonlight.

—Charles-Marie Leconte de Lisle, "The Black Panther"

"Where are you, Madame? Where have you gone?"

An explorer. He runs his hands under my down quilt. I'm not there. He searches. He loves that.

"Where are you, Madame?"

He moves forward in a tracking position, holding a flashlight in front of him to sweep away the darkness, left to right, right to left, all while creeping further under my sheets. He peers, pats, rummages, rearranges, excavates. But he doesn't find me.

"Where are you, Madame? Come out, where are you? Where is my little wild child? Are we hiding? Are we shy? Are we afraid of the explorer?"

The explorer's a little too committed to his role, with his pith helmet, his safari jacket, and his thick, tall socks. If he didn't have those rosy lips, those muscular shoulders, those plump calves, that mouthwatering body, so well-fleshed, I wouldn't have the patience.

"Watch out, Madame! The explorer's getting closer! Where's my wild child? Where's her little jungle? Come, Madame! Show yourself!"

In that instant, in one long, anxious snarl, with a yowl of impatience, fangs bared and glinting harshly, a black panther bounds out from under the bed. Me. I sink my claws into the explorer's back.

Explorers are so succulent. In spite of the long days spent trudging over inhospitable terrain, his hocks are still tender. His inner thigh is buttery soft to perfection. His shoulder is delectable. His belly is especially moist and rich. On top of that, the explorer is charming. Affectionate. A good sport. Perfect entertainment. He's almost as enjoyable as a rat. You catch him. Nip him playfully. Feel his heart beat faster. Let him go, let him flee. He thinks not long now until he's safe. Then, quickly, pin him. He struggles. Writhes. Let him run free once more. But you're already upon him. You taste his twitching flesh. You nibble him lightly. Release him. Recapture him. Until finally he surrenders. Exhausted and spent.

All of this is a game, to be sure. Purely for pleasure. After all, he's enjoying himself.

"Ah! Wild child! My wild child!"

The Beekeeper

I'm afraid of a kiss,
Like the kiss of a bee.
I turn and I toss,
I watch sleeplessly:
I'm afraid of a kiss!

—Paul Verlaine, *Songs Without Words*

I've fallen asleep beneath an immense thrum, at the heart of a droning swarm of bees.

A beekeeper is running toward me.

"Quick! Quick! Under my veil!"

His sharp eyes, very sharp, are fixed on me from behind the mesh because in the vegetable garden, surrounded by the sunflowers in bloom, near the straw-woven skeps sitting on their narrow shelf, I'm naked under the bees.

"Come!" he insists.

I'd always imagined that beekeepers were sealed head-to-toe in an unflattering white jumpsuit. But he's wearing absolutely nothing, except a wide hat with a veil hanging from the brim, and this veil, with eloquent, persuasive transparency, hangs to his feet.

"Come! In here! There's just enough room for two!"

As he speaks the words, he generously holds open a part of his veil and pulls me against himself under his wide-brimmed hat.

Outside, the bees are pushing against the veil. The pulsating swarm surges. A black mass, humming, ripples, rolls, throbs, darkens the daylight. The vibration swells, seething, relentless, resounding. Then I feel the thrust of one swift, searing prick.

The Astrologer

I saw the comet last night. Its tail is of a most impressive length; I pin some of my hopes on it.

—Madame de Sévigné, *Selected Letters*

I'm at the astrologer's. Across from me, under the lamp, in the silence contained by the curtains, bent over my star chart, with his enigmatic finger the astrologer traces the red and blue lines marking my destiny.

Suddenly, he straightens, snaps shut his copy of the ephemeris, pushes away his calculator, and turns his darkened eyes upon mine.

"We have quite a conjunction, Madame!" he gloats. "Quite a conjunction!"

As if he could distinguish—despite the drawn hangings—this captivating conjunction among the stars in the infinite sky, the astrologer blissfully lets his emerald eyes wander in the direction of the window.

His eyes re-alight on me.

"Your Venus is on my Mars, Madame!" he confides to me in a quivering voice, like the admission of a secret he can no longer rein in. "My Mars is on your Venus!"

I remain nonplussed. What I like about astrology are the stars, the planets, the celestial bodies. Not the astrologers.

However, as the man seated across from me, eyes shining, slowly leaves his chair, clearly intent on getting closer to me to better to explain the interesting implications of his cosmic revelation, a comet, head aflame, hurtles abruptly into the room, writhing like fire, sputtering, shattering windows and shutters. It sends papers and notes flying in every direction, snatches up the astrologer and his books in its whirling gust.

Flames flowing from its golden head, and followed by its blazing tail, blindingly bright, abandoning the astrologer where he lies stricken, the astral steed carries me to orbit.

The Sculptor

I am as lovely as a dream in stone;
My breast on which each finds his death in turn
Inspires the poet with a love as lone
As everlasting clay, and as taciturn.

—Charles Baudelaire, *The Flowers of Evil*

Tonight a sculptor, armed with hammer and chisel, is striking me brutally, striking and pounding and flailing without flagging. The blows are brutish. I am hard matter. But this man wants me, wants me completely.

It's thanks to him that that I begin to take shape, a rough outline of my bust materializes, my shoulders surface, my shapes emerge from the marble.

The sculptor examines me. I feel his callused hands inspecting my limbs, his fingers savoring my curves, his thumb tasting the arch of my back. He contemplates all the possibilities that are still contained within me, what I will become, what he wants me to be. He picks up his tools again, thrusts his gouge into me, and strikes, again and again and again.

At long last, there I am. It wasn't painless, but, in the end, I'm pleased with my sculptor. My neck is a thin, graceful arch. From my hair, pulled into a chignon, long curls have escaped here and there, and several fetching curls have fallen flirtatiously onto my exquisite shoulders. And my breasts, pert and round, are as charming as could have been imagined.

The artist considers his work. I stand bare under

his gaze, insolently immodest, exactly as he desires me. But I sense that he's preoccupied. He needs to perfect me and return to his work.

He takes his polishing stone and patiently smooths me, soothes me, strokes me. Under his tool, I feel my marble stir. I feel myself grow warm, silky, supple, alive. I arch my back and stretch. Exhilarated. Grateful.

My sculptor's hand slides over my hip, down to my legs, slips between my thighs, flattering, insistent, and fashions there at great length that impalpable place, the elements of pleasure, a liqueur, a slow heat building at my core. Open to his hand, eyes closed, I smile.

But what is he doing now? What has he chiseled there between my legs? Oh god! No! A fig leaf?!

The Climatologist

I find, close to you, the feeling of finally being in my true clime!

—Roger Martin du Gard, *The Thibaults*

Alessandro is a climatologist. A profession that, from all appearances, requires him to amble about completely naked. No doubt in order to discern without impediment the atmospheric conditions, to perceive any temperature variations with great precision, and to intimately appreciate the effects of wind and solar radiation.

The climatologist is quite pretty. Engaging expression. Italian smile. Molded and lavishly blessed with the fascinating physical attributes that a man enjoys at his prime. Rather shy, though, blushing a little as I examine him. Unfortunately quite fixated on his work. Completely preoccupied, currently, with the strength of currents.

"Do you know about the Gulf Stream?" inquires Alessandro, and already his eyes are shining. "The Gulf Stream! If you only knew! It's a very special current that comes from the Bahamas, from Florida. A river under the sea. Bluer than the water around it. Denser. And warmer, of course. Much warmer."

As he absentmindedly spins the imposing globe before us, the handsome Alessandro strokes the rotundity of the world with a contemplative hand, lingering over the enchanting azure of the oceans.

"Ah, the Gulf Stream!" he repeats, mesmerized. "A rolling heat! It passes over your body, it sucks you down, it carries you on, loses you in an eddy. Shall we go?"

And, leaning over the sphere spinning lazily before us, he grabs me by my waist and plunges with me madly into the Atlantic.

The Gulf Stream slams against us, ardent, impetuous. Alessandro presses me against his naked body.

"The Gulf Stream! Can you feel now?" he exults, as the blue swell pulls us faster, deeper. "Can you feel it?" he insists as he tightens his grip on me.

I feel it perfectly. To feel more fully would be impossible. The current's power is exceptional. Climatology, in the form of Alessandro, carries through on all of its promises.

The Executioner

One moment more, Mister Executioner, I beg you!

—Jeanne du Barry

My head is on the chopping block. It's uncomfortable. Fortunately, the executioner, hooded in black, has the body of an athlete, stationed close to me on two powerful Colossus legs.

From behind, black boots set off his thick calves. A short black tunic revealing formidable bare thighs. Black leather cuffs straining against muscular wrists. Deep-cut armholes gaping from his Herculean shoulders. Large, determined hands, which are holding the axe.

"Alright, Mister Executioner, alright, bring me death, but just a little one! Nick me ever so gently with the blade of your axe, but don't press down: that axe looks heavy, and I'm so bare, look at my thin, creamy skin—the blood runs beneath it, red and ready to pearl. Watch out for your flame, too! Yes, your torch. It's too close. Yes, it's burning me! It burns sublimely. I can feel it. Yes, that's it: let the flames brush me, let them lick me, yes. Look at my skin, though: it's getting red, I'll get hurt. Do you want to hurt me? You want to hurt me! You're a big brute of an executioner under your hood! A frightful executioner! What? What? No! I didn't mean it! You're not horrible. Put that blade away! You're even . . . very handsome. No, not the axe! The bones in my neck are minuscule. Such tiny bones. You'd pass through them without even having time to savor their crunch. So set down your axe, you're very charming, your eyes under your hood, your eyes, your smoldering eyes . . . Ah! That's better! It's so much better when you set down that axe. Frankly, you don't need it. You look much better without it. Now, what were we talking about? Oh, yes! Your eyes. Your smoldering eyes. But, all the same, wouldn't it be even better if I saw the rest of you? What are you hiding under that hood? A huge, nasty defect? A little imperfection that brings you shame? What? Ouch! Ah! Ahhh! Look what you've done to my head! Split! Gashed! All while it was lying so nicely on that feather pillow, dreaming of your large red hands!"

The Bishop

The Bishop of Rennes added to his good deeds the merit of hiding them sincerely and in good faith.

—Jean le Rond d'Alembert, *Éloges*

I'm kneeling in the darkness of a confessional where bright-burning eyes are fixed on me from the other side of the screen.

It's a man of the Church in purple robes. No doubt a dignitary. Maybe even a bishop. But bishops, I think to myself, are old. Can one so young be a bishop? With such eyes?

This man, for what it's worth, sports neither crosier nor miter. Only an ornate pectoral cross hanging over his mozzetta.

"My child, it's been reported to me by my clergy that you have a very beautiful soul," whispers the voice against the confessional screen. "I must examine this soul. I must pay reverence to it. It's of absolute necessity. Under the seal of confession, of course. In the utmost confidence. But it's dark here. And cramped. Let's go to your bed. We'll be better off there. But first, let me get more comfortable."

The bishop unbuttons his robes. Under the sheet, my soul shivers in anticipation of being consecrated, especially by a holy man, a man of God, a genuine specialist, even if, after removing his robes and the symbols of his station, the bishop currently resembles any other man, albeit a very attractive one, in ways that the cloth had concealed—a very attractive man with slim hips, firm thighs, and a divinely arched lower back.

"My mission in this lowly world, my child, consists of bringing to light what is hidden in darkness."

"Seek, seek, Monsieur. Nothing here is veiled that will not be unveiled."

And so, zealous and diligent, the bishop does seek, under the sheets, seeks oh-so-deeply and thoroughly. And my soul tastes these electrifying movements, draws back and crouches at the foot of the bed so that the search may continue further.

But men rush things. Even confessors. Suddenly:

"I see it! I see it! Ah, the minx, it's hiding. Don't move, I have it! Good Lord, it's a tender little thing! Oh, the little pussums! All atremble!"

His Excellency is satisfied.

"Very well, my child, very well. You possess a soul so exquisite that I am indebted to you for having bared it to me. Now, in the spirit of parity preached by our Holy Mother Church, I must make the oblation of mine unto you. I insist. It's highly encouraged by the last Vatican Council."

Without waiting, the prelate, obligingly, just as he would offer his amethyst ring for a kiss, extends to me his precious jewel, his ex-voto of love. *Behold the Lamb of God who takes away the sin from the world.*

The Beach Attendant

I heard a rake at the edge of the lawn
Make, among the murmuring gravel,
Its smooth purling sound.

—Anna de Noailles, *Les forces éternelles*
"Dans l'adolescence"

Those women who have never had the privilege of transforming into sand cannot conceive of the delight that such a metamorphosis delivers. Not just any sand, obviously. Not the fat yellow chunks heaped up on walkways. Nor the tired, moldering material where children loiter near the swings in the park. Not even that of dunes, or deserts, or rivers. Solely this silver-white sand, impalpable, shimmering beneath the sun in the blue sky, on a beach caressed by the sea.

I'm at the Tropezianna bar. It's early. The red- and white-striped lounge chairs lined up beside the water are still unoccupied. The beach attendant, Sergio, tan and magnificent, bustles around me, white polo, white belt, white teeth, white shorts clinging to his exquisite glutes and offering an unedited view of his obvious and generous virility.

"Come, Madame. I'll get you settled. This one should be to your liking."

Sergio shows me to the lounge chair he wants me laid out on. Before I recline, he checks the distribution of the padding in the cushion, turns it, turns it again, pats it, smooths it, brushes the dust off of it, and, with a meaningful look at me, flicks away a hair that had fallen there from his mane. Finally, after I've settled back, Sergio adjusts the umbrella above me, searches for the perfect position, offering me a low-angle view of his white shorts. Then he brings me mint water with ice, lots of ice, because the day will be hot, he warns me. Then he returns again, armed this time with a small rake, a curious tool with thin, soft teeth. He crouches close to me, and, with precise movements, so delicate and refined, he begins to rake the sand.

Instantly, I give a start. My skin trembles. A strange spasm, unfamiliar, runs through me. I am that white sand Sergio is combing through. That shifting substance, fleeting, elusive. That luminous sand. That immaterial material. I feel the little rake rasp at my soul. I am each grain. The minutest particle. I feel each clench, each tumble.

Sergio rakes on. Skillfully, artfully, he creates curls, whorls, winding, sinuous, and swirling like a Zen garden. At each movement, shivers ravish me.

But now he's stopping, and now he's standing up. The shorts approach at eye level.

"Something else, Madame? A refreshment?"

"Nothing at the moment, Sergio, thank you. Keep raking, please keep raking . . ."

The Clockmaker

It was the business of but a second; I would never have believed myself capable of such vigor.

—Alphonse Daudet, *Little Good-for-Nothing*

A clockmaker is busy at my nightstand, fiddling with my alarm clock. I turn to him, slightly uneasy in my sleep.

"Don't worry," he reassures me, "I'll wake you up. You'll be up at seven. You can count on me. Sleep. I always know what time it is. Also, listen, bring your ear closer: my heart beats the seconds. And feel my big hand. How precise it is. And my cogs. How regular they are. And my spring. How tight it is. Really, don't worry. My mechanism is in excellent working order. And I just wound it. Go on, sleep. I'll take care of everything. And you'll see—when I go off, my sound is loud and clear, perfect for the morning."

I fall back asleep then, and the clockmaker, to reassure me completely, steady like a metronome, punctiliously ticks brief kisses from my throat to my ankles, here, there, second by second.

The clockmaker's eagerness escalates, however. Despite my sleep, which I'd prefer to be deeper, I sense that time is intensifying. The seconds accelerate. The mechanism has sprung, whirring out of control. The clockmaker's on the fritz. He's going off much too early. He's going off in the middle of the night.

And what a sound!

The Burglar

'Tis the hour, O gay dancer, midnight laughs,
its come-hither glance illumined under its mask.

—Victor Hugo, *The Legend of the Ages*

A dark breeze, coming in from the window this evening, moves across my room. It's a burglar in a black catsuit. I barely have time to make out his form before he's upon me, fast as the storm, eddying the air with a sweep of his cape. And his eyes overpower me from behind his black satin mask.

I cry out.

"Help! Somebody help!"

He knows how to quiet me. His lips are scalding, and his tongue probes deep. Through the cutouts in his silken mask, I see his eyes gleam.

"I am your thief."

His warm voice slinks past my ear.

"And I've come to claim the key that unlocks your dreams."

The silk-encircled eyes never release mine, carry me with them through the open window, fly me through the night, lead me through the dark to where dreams reside.

MICHAL AJVAZ, *The Golden Age.*
The Other City.

PIERRE ALBERT-BIROT, *Grabinoulor.*

YUZ ALESHKOVSKY, *Kangaroo.*

FELIPE ALFAU, *Chromos.*
Locos.

JOE AMATO, *Samuel Taylor's Last Night.*

IVAN ÂNGELO, *The Celebration.*
The Tower of Glass.

ANTÓNIO LOBO ANTUNES, *Knowledge of Hell.*
The Splendor of Portugal.

ALAIN ARIAS-MISSON, *Theatre of Incest.*

JOHN ASHBERY & JAMES SCHUYLER, *A Nest of Ninnies.*

ROBERT ASHLEY, *Perfect Lives.*

GABRIELA AVIGUR-ROTEM, *Heatwave and Crazy Birds.*

DJUNA BARNES, *Ladies Almanack.*
Ryder.

JOHN BARTH, *Letters.*
Sabbatical.

DONALD BARTHELME, *The King.*
Paradise.

SVETISLAV BASARA, *Chinese Letter.*

MIQUEL BAUÇÀ, *The Siege in the Room.*

RENÉ BELLETTO, *Dying.*

MAREK BIENCZYK, *Transparency.*

ANDREI BITOV, *Pushkin House.*

ANDREJ BLATNIK, *You Do Understand.*
Law of Desire.

LOUIS PAUL BOON, *Chapel Road.*
My Little War.
Summer in Termuren.

ROGER BOYLAN, *Killoyle.*

IGNÁCIO DE LOYOLA BRANDÃO, *Anonymous Celebrity.*
Zero.

BONNIE BREMSER, *Troia: Mexican Memoirs.*

CHRISTINE BROOKE-ROSE, *Amalgamemnon.*

BRIGID BROPHY, *In Transit.*
The Prancing Novelist.

GERALD L. BRUNS, *Modern Poetry and the Idea of Language.*

GABRIELLE BURTON, *Heartbreak Hotel.*

MICHEL BUTOR, *Degrees.*
Mobile.

G. CABRERA INFANTE, *Infante's Inferno.*
Three Trapped Tigers.

JULIETA CAMPOS, *The Fear of Losing Eurydice.*

ANNE CARSON, *Eros the Bittersweet.*

ORLY CASTEL-BLOOM, *Dolly City.*

LOUIS-FERDINAND CÉLINE, *North.*
Conversations with Professor Y.
London Bridge.

MARIE CHAIX, *The Laurels of Lake Constance.*

HUGO CHARTERIS, *The Tide Is Right.*

ERIC CHEVILLARD, *Demolishing Nisard.*
The Author and Me.

MARC CHOLODENKO, *Mordechai Schamz.*

JOSHUA COHEN, *Witz.*

EMILY HOLMES COLEMAN, *The Shutter of Snow.*

ERIC CHEVILLARD, *The Author and Me.*

ROBERT COOVER, *A Night at the Movies.*

STANLEY CRAWFORD, *Log of the S.S. The Mrs Unguentine.*
Some Instructions to My Wife.

RENÉ CREVEL, *Putting My Foot in It.*

RALPH CUSACK, *Cadenza.*

NICHOLAS DELBANCO, *Sherbrookes.*
The Count of Concord.

NIGEL DENNIS, *Cards of Identity.*

PETER DIMOCK, *A Short Rhetoric for Leaving the Family.*

ARIEL DORFMAN, *Konfidenz.*

COLEMAN DOWELL, *Island People.*
Too Much Flesh and Jabez.

ARKADII DRAGOMOSHCHENKO, *Dust.*

RIKKI DUCORNET, *Phosphor in Dreamland.*
The Complete Butcher's Tales.

RIKKI DUCORNET (cont.), *The Jade Cabinet*.
The Fountains of Neptune.

WILLIAM EASTLAKE, *The Bamboo Bed*.
Castle Keep.
Lyric of the Circle Heart.

JEAN ECHENOZ, *Chopin's Move*.

STANLEY ELKIN, *A Bad Man*.
Criers and Kibitzers, Kibitzers and Criers.
The Dick Gibson Show.
The Franchiser.
The Living End.
Mrs. Ted Bliss.

FRANÇOIS EMMANUEL, *Invitation to a Voyage*.

PAUL EMOND, *The Dance of a Sham*.

SALVADOR ESPRIU, *Ariadne in the Grotesque Labyrinth*.

LESLIE A. FIEDLER, *Love and Death in the American Novel*.

JUAN FILLOY, *Op Oloop*.

ANDY FITCH, *Pop Poetics*.

GUSTAVE FLAUBERT, *Bouvard and Pécuchet*.

KASS FLEISHER, *Talking out of School*.

JON FOSSE, *Aliss at the Fire*.
Melancholy.

FORD MADOX FORD, *The March of Literature*.

MAX FRISCH, *I'm Not Stiller*.
Man in the Holocene.

CARLOS FUENTES, *Christopher Unborn*.
Distant Relations.
Terra Nostra.
Where the Air Is Clear.

TAKEHIKO FUKUNAGA, *Flowers of Grass*.

WILLIAM GADDIS, JR., *The Recognitions*.

JANICE GALLOWAY, *Foreign Parts*.
The Trick Is to Keep Breathing.

WILLIAM H. GASS, *Life Sentences*.
The Tunnel.
The World Within the Word.
Willie Masters' Lonesome Wife.

GÉRARD GAVARRY, *Hoppla! 1 2 3*.

ETIENNE GILSON, *The Arts of the Beautiful*.
Forms and Substances in the Arts.

C. S. GISCOMBE, *Giscome Road*.
Here.

DOUGLAS GLOVER, *Bad News of the Heart*.

WITOLD GOMBROWICZ, *A Kind of Testament*.

PAULO EMÍLIO SALES GOMES, *P's Three Women*.

GEORGI GOSPODINOV, *Natural Novel*.

JUAN GOYTISOLO, *Count Julian*.
Juan the Landless.
Makbara.
Marks of Identity.

HENRY GREEN, *Blindness*.
Concluding.
Doting.
Nothing.

JACK GREEN, *Fire the Bastards!*

JIŘÍ GRUŠA, *The Questionnaire*.

MELA HARTWIG, *Am I a Redundant Human Being?*

JOHN HAWKES, *The Passion Artist*.
Whistlejacket.

ELIZABETH HEIGHWAY, ED., *Contemporary Georgian Fiction*.

AIDAN HIGGINS, *Balcony of Europe*.
Blind Man's Bluff.
Bornholm Night-Ferry.
Langrishe, Go Down.
Scenes from a Receding Past.

KEIZO HINO, *Isle of Dreams*.

KAZUSHI HOSAKA, *Plainsong*.

ALDOUS HUXLEY, *Antic Hay*.
Point Counter Point.
Those Barren Leaves.
Time Must Have a Stop.

NAOYUKI II, *The Shadow of a Blue Cat*.

DRAGO JANČAR, *The Tree with No Name*.

MIKHEIL JAVAKHISHVILI, *Kvachi*.

GERT JONKE, *The Distant Sound*.
Homage to Czerny.
The System of Vienna.

JACQUES JOUET, *Mountain R.*
Savage.
Upstaged.

MIEKO KANAI, *The Word Book.*

YORAM KANIUK, *Life on Sandpaper.*

ZURAB KARUMIDZE, *Dagny.*

JOHN KELLY, *From Out of the City.*

HUGH KENNER, *Flaubert, Joyce
and Beckett: The Stoic Comedians.*
Joyce's Voices.

DANILO KIŠ, *The Attic.*
The Lute and the Scars.
Psalm 44.
A Tomb for Boris Davidovich.

ANITA KONKKA, *A Fool's Paradise.*

GEORGE KONRÁD, *The City Builder.*

TADEUSZ KONWICKI, *A Minor
Apocalypse.*
The Polish Complex.

ANNA KORDZAIA-SAMADASHVILI,
Me, Margarita.

MENIS KOUMANDAREAS, *Koula.*

ELAINE KRAF, *The Princess of 72nd Street.*

JIM KRUSOE, *Iceland.*

AYSE KULIN, *Farewell: A Mansion in
Occupied Istanbul.*

EMILIO LASCANO TEGUI, *On Elegance
While Sleeping.*

ERIC LAURRENT, *Do Not Touch.*

VIOLETTE LEDUC, *La Bâtarde.*

EDOUARD LEVÉ, *Autoportrait.*
Newspaper.
Suicide.
Works.

MARIO LEVI, *Istanbul Was a Fairy Tale.*

DEBORAH LEVY, *Billy and Girl.*

JOSÉ LEZAMA LIMA, *Paradiso.*

ROSA LIKSOM, *Dark Paradise.*

OSMAN LINS, *Avalovara.*
The Queen of the Prisons of Greece.

FLORIAN LIPUŠ, *The Errors of Young Tjaž.*

GORDON LISH, *Peru.*

ALF MACLOCHLAINN, *Out of Focus.*
Past Habitual.

The Corpus in the Library.

RON LOEWINSOHN, *Magnetic Field(s).*

YURI LOTMAN, *Non-Memoirs.*

D. KEITH MANO, *Take Five.*

MINA LOY, *Stories and Essays of Mina Loy.*

MICHELINE AHARONIAN MARCOM,
A Brief History of Yes.
The Mirror in the Well.

BEN MARCUS, *The Age of Wire and String.*

WALLACE MARKFIELD, *Teitlebaum's
Window.*

DAVID MARKSON, *Reader's Block.*
Wittgenstein's Mistress.

CAROLE MASO, *AVA.*

HISAKI MATSUURA, *Triangle.*

LADISLAV MATEJKA & KRYSTYNA
POMORSKA, EDS., *Readings in Russian
Poetics: Formalist & Structuralist Views.*

HARRY MATHEWS, *Cigarettes.*
The Conversions.
The Human Country.
The Journalist.
My Life in CIA.
Singular Pleasures.
The Sinking of the Odradek.
Stadium.
Tlooth.

HISAKI MATSUURA, *Triangle.*

DONAL MCLAUGHLIN, *beheading the
virgin mary, and other stories.*

JOSEPH MCELROY, *Night Soul and
Other Stories.*

ABDELWAHAB MEDDEB, *Talismano.*

GERHARD MEIER, *Isle of the Dead.*

HERMAN MELVILLE, *The Confidence-
Man.*

AMANDA MICHALOPOULOU, *I'd Like.*

STEVEN MILLHAUSER, *The Barnum
Museum.*
In the Penny Arcade.

RALPH J. MILLS, JR., *Essays on Poetry.*

MOMUS, *The Book of Jokes.*

CHRISTINE MONTALBETTI, *The Origin
of Man.*
Western.

NICHOLAS MOSLEY, *Accident.*
Assassins.
Catastrophe Practice.
A Garden of Trees.
Hopeful Monsters.
Imago Bird.
Inventing God.
Look at the Dark.
Metamorphosis.
Natalie Natalia.
Serpent.

WARREN MOTTE, *Fables of the Novel: French Fiction since 1990.*
Fiction Now: The French Novel in the 21st Century.
Mirror Gazing.
Oulipo: A Primer of Potential Literature.

GERALD MURNANE, *Barley Patch.*
Inland.

YVES NAVARRE, *Our Share of Time.*
Sweet Tooth.

DOROTHY NELSON, *In Night's City.*
Tar and Feathers.

ESHKOL NEVO, *Homesick.*

WILFRIDO D. NOLLEDO, *But for the Lovers.*

BORIS A. NOVAK, *The Master of Insomnia.*

FLANN O'BRIEN, *At Swim-Two-Birds.*
The Best of Myles.
The Dalkey Archive.
The Hard Life.
The Poor Mouth.
The Third Policeman.

CLAUDE OLLIER, *The Mise-en-Scène.*
Wert and the Life Without End.

PATRIK OUŘEDNÍK, *Europeana.*
The Opportune Moment, 1855.

BORIS PAHOR, *Necropolis.*

FERNANDO DEL PASO, *News from the Empire.*
Palinuro of Mexico.

ROBERT PINGET, *The Inquisitory.*
Mahu or The Material.
Trio.

MANUEL PUIG, *Betrayed by Rita Hayworth.*
The Buenos Aires Affair.
Heartbreak Tango.

RAYMOND QUENEAU, *The Last Days.*
Odile.
Pierrot Mon Ami.
Saint Glinglin.

ANN QUIN, *Berg.*
Passages.
Three.
Tripticks.

ISHMAEL REED, *The Free-Lance Pallbearers.*
The Last Days of Louisiana Red.
Ishmael Reed: The Plays.
Juice!
The Terrible Threes.
The Terrible Twos.
Yellow Back Radio Broke-Down.

JASIA REICHARDT, *15 Journeys Warsaw to London.*

JOÃO UBALDO RIBEIRO, *House of the Fortunate Buddhas.*

JEAN RICARDOU, *Place Names.*

RAINER MARIA RILKE,
The Notebooks of Malte Laurids Brigge.

JULIÁN RÍOS, *The House of Ulysses.*
Larva: A Midsummer Night's Babel.
Poundemonium.

ALAIN ROBBE-GRILLET, *Project for a Revolution in New York.*
A Sentimental Novel.

AUGUSTO ROA BASTOS, *I the Supreme.*

DANIËL ROBBERECHTS, *Arriving in Avignon.*

JEAN ROLIN, *The Explosion of the Radiator Hose.*

OLIVIER ROLIN, *Hotel Crystal.*

ALIX CLEO ROUBAUD, *Alix's Journal.*

JACQUES ROUBAUD, *The Form of a City Changes Faster, Alas, Than the Human Heart.*
The Great Fire of London.
Hortense in Exile.
Hortense Is Abducted.
Mathematics: The Plurality of Worlds of Lewis.
Some Thing Black.

FOR A FULL LIST OF PUBLICATIONS, VISIT: www.dalkeyarchive.com

RAYMOND ROUSSEL, *Impressions of Africa.*

VEDRANA RUDAN, *Night.*

PABLO M. RUIZ, *Four Cold Chapters on the Possibility of Literature.*

GERMAN SADULAEV, *The Maya Pill.*

TOMAŽ ŠALAMUN, *Soy Realidad.*

LYDIE SALVAYRE, *The Company of Ghosts.*
The Lecture.
The Power of Flies.

LUIS RAFAEL SÁNCHEZ, *Macho Camacho's Beat.*

SEVERO SARDUY, *Cobra & Maitreya.*

NATHALIE SARRAUTE, *Do You Hear Them?*
Martereau.
The Planetarium.

STIG SÆTERBAKKEN, *Siamese.*
Self-Control.
Through the Night.

ARNO SCHMIDT, *Collected Novellas.*
Collected Stories.
Nobodaddy's Children.
Two Novels.

ASAF SCHURR, *Motti.*

GAIL SCOTT, *My Paris.*

DAMION SEARLS, *What We Were Doing and Where We Were Going.*

JUNE AKERS SEESE,
Is This What Other Women Feel Too?

BERNARD SHARE, *Inish.*
Transit.

VIKTOR SHKLOVSKY, *Bowstring.*
Literature and Cinematography.
Theory of Prose.
Third Factory.
Zoo, or Letters Not about Love.

PIERRE SINIAC, *The Collaborators.*

KJERSTI A. SKOMSVOLD,
The Faster I Walk, the Smaller I Am.

JOSEF ŠKVORECKÝ, *The Engineer of Human Souls.*

GILBERT SORRENTINO, *Aberration of Starlight.*
Blue Pastoral.
Crystal Vision.

Imaginative Qualities of Actual Things.
Mulligan Stew. Red the Fiend.
Steelwork.
Under the Shadow.

MARKO SOSIČ, *Ballerina, Ballerina.*

ANDRZEJ STASIUK, *Dukla.*
Fado.

GERTRUDE STEIN, *The Making of Americans.*
A Novel of Thank You.

LARS SVENDSEN, *A Philosophy of Evil.*

PIOTR SZEWC, *Annihilation.*

GONÇALO M. TAVARES, *A Man: Klaus Klump.*
Jerusalem.
Learning to Pray in the Age of Technique.

LUCIAN DAN TEODOROVICI,
Our Circus Presents...

NIKANOR TERATOLOGEN, *Assisted Living.*

STEFAN THEMERSON, *Hobson's Island.*
The Mystery of the Sardine.
Tom Harris.

TAEKO TOMIOKA, *Building Waves.*

JOHN TOOMEY, *Sleepwalker.*

DUMITRU TSEPENEAG, *Hotel Europa.*
The Necessary Marriage.
Pigeon Post.
Vain Art of the Fugue.

ESTHER TUSQUETS, *Stranded.*

DUBRAVKA UGRESIC, *Lend Me Your Character.*
Thank You for Not Reading.

TOR ULVEN, *Replacement.*

MATI UNT, *Brecht at Night.*
Diary of a Blood Donor.
Things in the Night.

ÁLVARO URIBE & OLIVIA SEARS, EDS.,
Best of Contemporary Mexican Fiction.

ELOY URROZ, *Friction.*
The Obstacles.

LUISA VALENZUELA, *Dark Desires and the Others.*
He Who Searches.

PAUL VERHAEGHEN, *Omega Minor.*

BORIS VIAN, *Heartsnatcher.*

LLORENÇ VILLALONGA, *The Dolls' Room.*

TOOMAS VINT, *An Unending Landscape.*

ORNELA VORPSI, *The Country Where No One Ever Dies.*

AUSTRYN WAINHOUSE, *Hedyphagetica.*

CURTIS WHITE, *America's Magic Mountain.*
The Idea of Home.
Memories of My Father Watching TV.
Requiem.

DIANE WILLIAMS,
Excitability: Selected Stories.
Romancer Erector.

DOUGLAS WOOLF, *Wall to Wall.*
Ya! & John-Juan.

JAY WRIGHT, *Polynomials and Pollen.*
The Presentable Art of Reading Absence.

PHILIP WYLIE, *Generation of Vipers.*

MARGUERITE YOUNG, *Angel in the Forest.*
Miss MacIntosh, My Darling.

REYOUNG, *Unbabbling.*

VLADO ŽABOT, *The Succubus.*

ZORAN ŽIVKOVIĆ , *Hidden Camera.*

LOUIS ZUKOFSKY, *Collected Fiction.*

VITOMIL ZUPAN, *Minuet for Guitar.*

SCOTT ZWIREN, *God Head.*

AND MORE . . .